Muppet Babies and character names are trademarks of Henson Associates, Inc.
© Henson Associates, Inc., 1987.

Published by

GRANDREAMS LIMITED,
Jadwin House,
205/211, Kentish Town Road,
London NW5 2JU.

Printed in Holland.

ISBN 0 86227 478 8

Contents

In Search of the Great White Soap

The Muppet Babies had just come in from playing in the sand-pit, and they were very dirty. It was time for their baths.

"Who's going first?" Nanny asked.

"Oh, I will, Nanny," Piggy piped up. "I love being clean!"

"I'm next!" Scooter chimed in.

"Then me!" Skeeter added.

"Bath! Bath!" Animal jumped up and down, leaving muddy footprints all over the nursery.

"Then it's my turn," Fozzie said.

Gonzo was next. "And mine!"

"And mine!" Rowlf called.

"That leaves you, Kermit," Nanny said. "I want you all to be as clean as clean can be before you go to sleep tonight."

"Yes, Nanny," Kermit agreed. "I'll have my bath as soon as everyone else has finished."

"That's fine," Nanny smiled. "I'll be back to tuck you in for the night." Then she closed the door behind her.

One by one, the Muppet Babies had their baths. One by one they put on clean pyjamas and climbed into bed.

Then it was Kermit's turn.

Kermit loved his bath. Maybe that was because he always had lots of company. There was his rubber duck, his rubber whale, his mermaid, his pirate ship, and best of all, there was his own toy boat, the *Silver Frog*. Captain Kermit had many an exciting adventure aboard the *Silver Frog*.

Kermit stepped into the bath, which was filled with warm water. There was a new bar of white soap waiting for him. He took his flannel in one hand and the soap in the other and started rubbing and scrubbing. Then suddenly the soap squirted out of his hand and went floating away!

"Soap overboard!" called Captain Kermit. Baby Kermit always became Captain Kermit as soon as it seemed a new adventure was about to begin. He looked through his telescope. He could see the soap floating away. So he raised the sails of his ship and went in pursuit of the Great White Soap.

Captain Kermit followed the soap for miles and miles. The wind was high, and waves splashed over the sides of the *Silver Frog*. He searched to the north, south, east, and west, but the Great White Soap was not to be found.

"Oh, no!" Kermit thought. "If I can't find the soap, I can't wash, and Nanny will be cross with me. She wanted me to be as clean as clean can be before I went to sleep!"

So Kermit sailed on. He was still looking for the Great White Soap when he spotted an island through his telescope.

Same

8

"That would be a good place to drop anchor and dry off for a while," he decided. So he sailed to the island and anchored his boat in a calm pool of water.

Floating in the water was a duck. "I am in search of a large white bar of soap," Captain Kermit told him. "Have you seen it go by?"

"Quack! Quack, quack, quack!" answered the duck, pointing with one of its wings in the direction of a narrow channel. In duck talk that means: "I did see a medium-sized bar of soap. It went that-a-way."

"Thanks," Kermit said politely, tipping his captain's hat.

Kermit hopped off the *Silver Frog* and waded onto the island. He lunched on coconuts and bananas, and filled the coconut shell with some cool water from a small stream. Then he boarded the ship again, brushed his teeth, pulled up his anchor, and set his course for the narrow channel.

There were high cliffs on both sides of the channel. It was so narrow that once the *Silver Frog* had sailed in, there was no way to turn around. So Captain Kermit kept going straight ahead. He was looking for the soap through his telescope when he saw something right in front of him. It was great, all right — but it was a great *grey whale!* The whale was spouting a stream of water and swimming straight for the *Silver Frog*.

"Yipes!" shouted Captain Kermit. With a flip of its giant tail, the whale dived under the water, lifting the little boat on its back. The *Silver Frog* rocked from side to side.

"Oh, oh! Oh, no!" Captain Kermit cried as he slid from one side of the boat to the other. "Frog overboard!"

Captain Kermit slid right into the water.

Kermit swam under the waves, down and down and down. He passed the whale, who nodded and smiled at him with a mouthful of great white teeth. As he swam, Kermit saw blue fish and red fish and yellow fish. He saw pink coral reefs and a plump pink mermaid. But he saw no sign of the Great White Soap.

"Have you seen a large white soap floating by?" Captain Kermit asked the mermaid.

"Sorry," she replied. "I've only seen a smallish white soap. But since you're down here, would you like to stay to tea?"

The mermaid was very beautiful, and Captain Kermit could not refuse. So he and the mermaid had tea at the bottom of the ocean. She served the tea in her very best cups and saucers. With the tea came homemade biscuits.

When Kermit had finished every drop of the tea and had eaten three biscuits (which were quite soggy, but still tasty), he thanked

the mermaid for her hospitality. Then he swam up to the surface again, still in search of the Great White Soap.

The *Silver Frog* was rocking gently in the water. But anchored next to it was a pirate ship, flying a special school crossing flag.

"Shouldn't that be a skull and crossbones flag?" Captain Kermit asked the pirate king.

"Not on the *Jolly Gonzo*!" the pirate king replied. "This ship is dedicated to education and road safety! Now shiver your timbers and ho-ho-ho. It's time to walk the plank!"

"But I'm already in the water," Kermit reminded him.

"That's true," said the pirate king.

"Have you seen the Great White Soap?" Captain Kermit inquired.

"No," replied the pirate king. "But I did notice a sliver of soap when I pulled in here. It floated over there."

"Thank you," said Captain Kermit, and he began to swim to where the pirate king had pointed. He swam and he swam and he swam, until he swam right into something floating in the water.

Kermit crossed his eyes and squinted. It was the Great White Soap! Only it wasn't great anymore—it was a very little bit of white soap. And as Captain Kermit watched, it totally disappeared.

"Oh, no!" Captain Kermit cried. "The Great White Soap has vanished! What am I going to do? I'll never be able to wash now!"

"Kermit!" said a familiar voice. Kermit looked up in surprise. There was Nanny, standing over the bath with a towel in her hands. "You've been rubbing and scrubbing so hard, you've used up all the soap! I think you're clean enough, don't you? Time to dry off and get into bed!"

Kermit looked around. There was his flannel, his rubber duck, his rubber whale, his mermaid, his toy pirate ship, and the *Silver Frog*. The bath was full of soap suds, and Kermit was as clean as clean can be.

"So that's what happened to the soap," he said. He climbed out of the bath, dried off, put on his pyjamas, and got into bed. Nanny tucked him in.

"Good night, Babies!" she called as she turned off the light.

"Good night, Nanny!" the Muppet Babies chorused.

Baby Kermit wiggled and snuggled down under the covers. He wanted to think about his adventure in the *Silver Frog*. But before he could remember how it all began, he was fast asleep!

BABY GONZO IS CONFUSED

Baby Gonzo has not been able to count the triangles on this page. Can you? Answer at foot of page.

16

THE TREASURE HUNT

Baby Kermit and Baby Piggy are preparing for a treasure hunt. Perhaps you can help them find their way through the maze to the centre and the treasure.

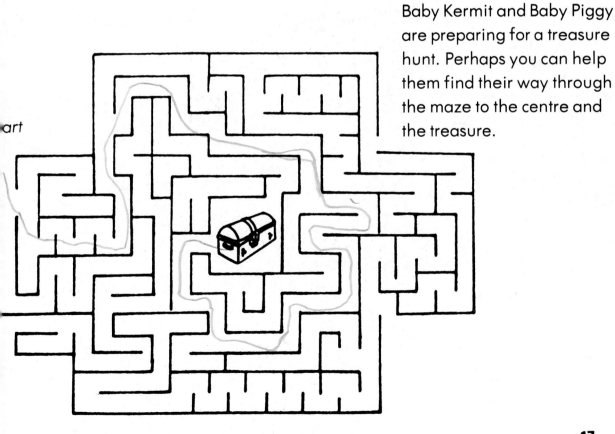

art

THE DICE GAME

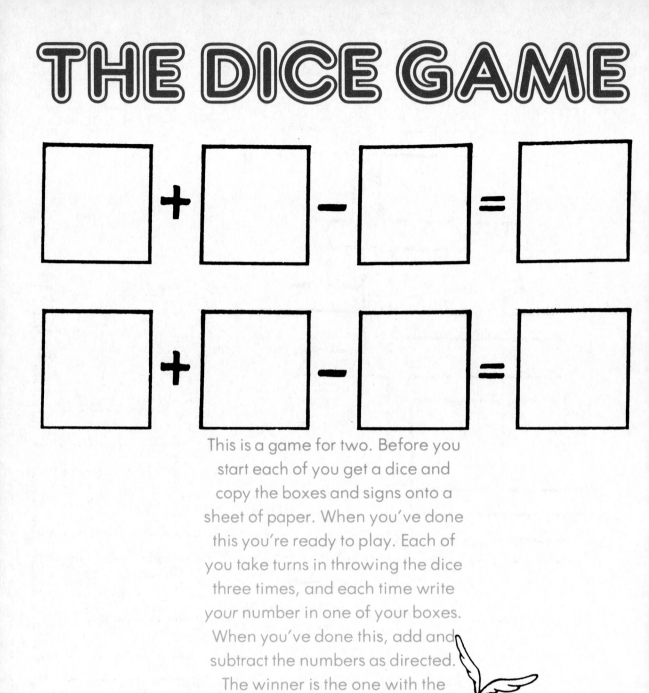

This is a game for two. Before you start each of you get a dice and copy the boxes and signs onto a sheet of paper. When you've done this you're ready to play. Each of you take turns in throwing the dice three times, and each time write your number in one of your boxes. When you've done this, add and subtract the numbers as directed. The winner is the one with the largest result.

HELP BABY ANIMAL

Baby Animal cannot find his way out of the maze and Baby Piggy wants to go and fetch him. But which way should she go?

19

TO COLOUR

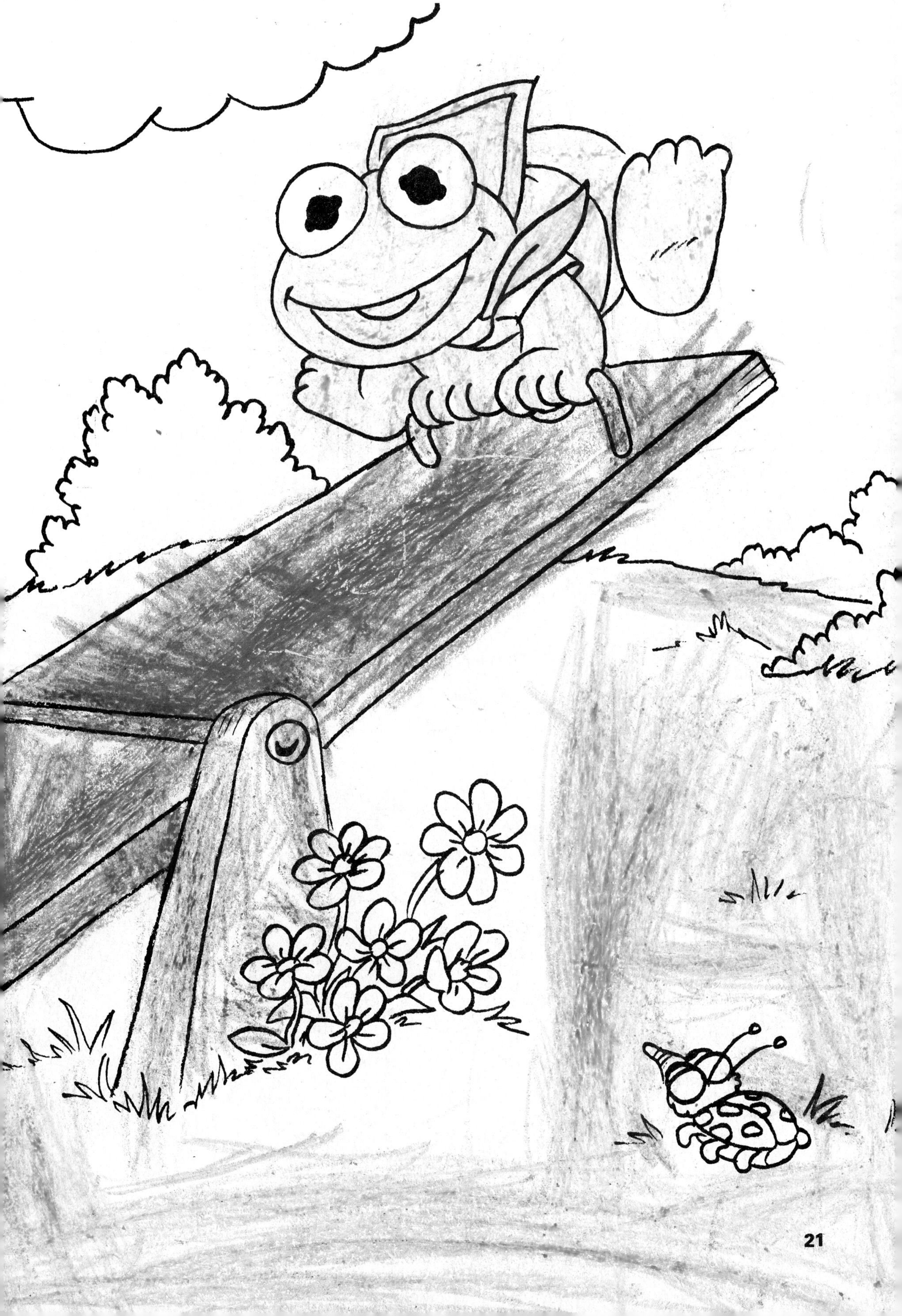

MARY, MARY, QUITE CONTRARY

Mary, Mary, quite contrary,
How does your garden grow?
With silver bells and cockle shells,
And pretty maids all in a row.

LADYBIRD, LADYBIRD, FLY AWAY HOME

Ladybird, ladybird,
Fly away home,
Your house is on fire
And your children are gone;
All except one,
And that's little Ann,
And she has crept under
The warming pan.

SEESAW, MARGERY DAW

Seesaw, Margery Daw,
Jacky shall have a new master;
Jacky shall have but a penny a day,
Because he can't work any faster.

RING AROUND THE ROSES

Ring around the roses,
A pocket full of posies,
A-tishoo! A-tishoo!
We all fall down.

THE DRAGON

Draw the picture above in the grid below, using the squares as a
guide. Then colour both pictures in.

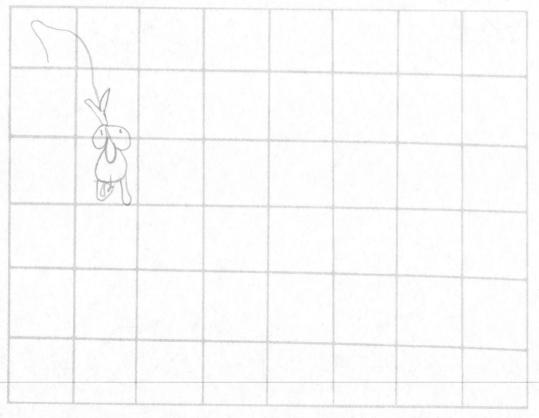

LEAF GAME

Baby Skeeter likes dancing among the leaves. Only two leaves are the same. See if you can find them.

Answer: 1 & 6

LITTLE TOMMY TUCKER

Little Tommy Tucker
Sings for his supper.
What shall we give him?
White bread and butter.
How shall he cut it
Without a knife?
How will he be married
Without a wife?

PAT-A-CAKE

Pat-a-cake, pat-a-cake, baker's man,
Bake me a cake as fast as you can;
Pat it and prick it, and mark it with B,
Put it in the oven for baby and me.

Little Bo-Peep has lost her sheep,
And doesn't know where to find them;
Leave them alone, and they'll come home,
Wagging their tails behind them.

LITTLE BOY BLUE

Little Boy Blue,
Come blow your horn,
The sheep's in the meadow,
The cow's in the corn;
But where is the little boy
Who looks after the sheep?
He's under a haystack
Fast asleep.
Will you wake him?
No, not I,
For if I do,
He's sure to cry.

GONZO'S MAZE

Gonzo wants to see Piggy. Can you help him find a path across the maze?

SPOT THE DIFFERENCE

Can you find the 5 differences between the two drawings?

BUTTERFLIES

1

5

2

6

3

2 of these butterflies are the same. Which ones?

4

BALL WORDSEARCH

R	U	G	Y	—	F	A	O	G	Y	B	U	R
A	S	K	E	T	F	O	O	T	H	A	N	R	U
S	—	A	H	F	O	O	V	B	A	N	O	U	G
—	B	A	A	L	—	B	O	O	N	B	O	G	Y
H	A	N	D	—	B	A	L	L	O	U	—	B	—
A	L	E	Y	B	A	S	L	U	R	G	B	Y	B
N	L	—	B	A	S	K	E	Y	—	B	A	L	A
T	B	A	S	G	V	K	E	B	B	G	Y	L	A	L
H	A	N	—	B	O	B	T	A	R	U	G	L	O	L
O	L	L	E	Y	L	L	—	R	U	G	B	A	S	K
O	R	A	Y	O	D	—	B	A	L	L	Y	T	A	T
R	U	G	B	T	—	B	A	L	L	F	O	O	T	—
U	G	B	A	—	B	R	L	U	V	O	L	O	F	B
B	A	S	K	B	O	U	L	G	B	O	O	T	O	A
Y	F	O	O	F	B	A	S	B	Y	T	B	O	O	L
—	V	O	V	O	L	L	E	Y	—	B	A	L	L	L
B	A	F	O	O	T	Y	Y	—	B	A	L	U	G	H
A	F	O	O	T	—	V	O	B	O	L	Y	G	B	A
L	T	O	L	—	H	A	N	A	O	L	—	B	A	N
L	O	T	Y	R	U	G	U	R	B	Y	R	Y	B	D

Can you find the names of 5 ball games hidden amongst the letters? Baby Animal has written them two ways, from left to right and up and down.

HICKETY, PICKETY, MY BLACK HEN

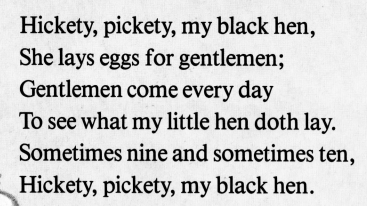

Hickety, pickety, my black hen,
She lays eggs for gentlemen;
Gentlemen come every day
To see what my little hen doth lay.
Sometimes nine and sometimes ten,
Hickety, pickety, my black hen.

LITTLE TOMMY TITTLEMOUSE

Little Tommy Tittlemouse
Lived in a little house;
He caught fishes
In other men's ditches.

THE GRAND OLD DUKE OF YORK

Oh, the grand Old Duke of York,
He had ten thousand men;
He marched them up to the top of the hill,
And he marched them down again.
And when they were up, they were up,
And when they were down, they were down,
And when they were only halfway up,
They were neither up nor down.

RIDE A COCK-HORSE TO BANBURY CROSS

Ride a cock-horse to Banbury Cross,

To see a fine lady upon a white horse;

Rings on her fingers and bells on her toes,

She shall have music wherever she goes.

A PICTURE TO COPY

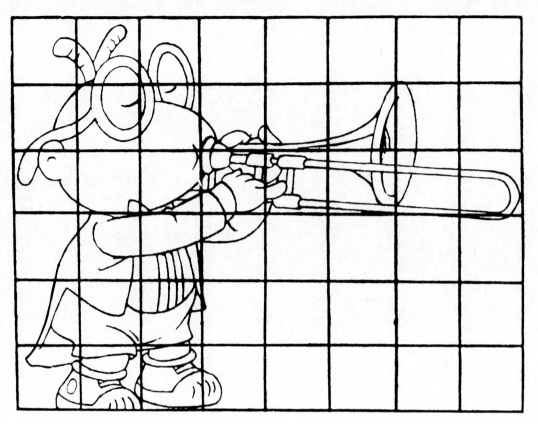

Draw Scooter with the help of the grid below.

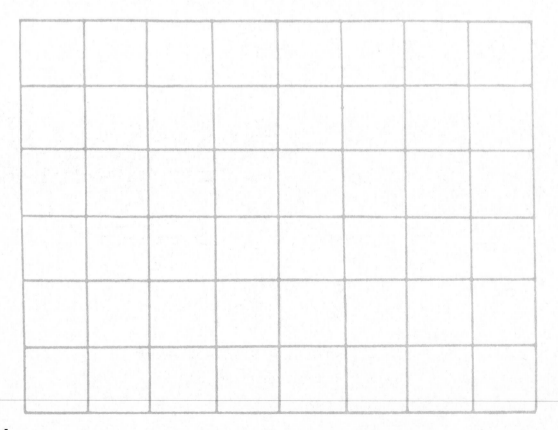

SPOT THE DIFFERENCE

When this drawing was being copied
the artist made 5 mistakes. See if you
can find them.

Beyond the Broccoli Forest

It was a lovely day. Outside the nursery window the sky was blue, the birds were chirping, and the squirrels were scampering to and fro. Inside the nursery, Nanny was serving lunch. Baby Piggy sat staring down into a plate of steaming broccoli.

"Must I eat this?" she asked, wrinkling up her pretty pink nose.

"But, Piggy," said Nanny, "I thought you liked broccoli?"

"I did—yesterday. But today," she stole a look at Skeeter's and Scooter's plates, "I would much rather have macaroni cheese like them."

"But I thought you didn't like macaroni cheese?" said the ever-patient Nanny.

"That was last Wednesday, but today it looks nice. Or maybe I could eat some of Fozzie's mashed potatoes and peas?"

"Don't you remember, Piggy?" asked Fozzie. "Last Saturday you said you didn't like the lumps. Although I think the lumps are the best part."

"Hmm..." said Piggy. "Then I'll have tomato soup with bread, like Kermie."

"On Tuesday you said red was a weird colour for soup," Kermit reminded her.

"I did? Then give me what Gonzo has," she said.

Gonzo pushed his plate toward Piggy. "Here, you can have half of my ketchup and asparagus sandwich. Help yourself."

"No, thank you," Piggy said quickly. "Can't I have my chocolate pudding now, Nanny? Pretty please?"

"Not until you have finished everything on your plate," Nanny said firmly. "That goes for the rest of you too. Eat up, children."

Nanny left the nursery.

Piggy looked down into her plate at the heap of broccoli just sitting there waiting for her to eat it.

"How am I ever going to finish all of that?" she wondered aloud. She stared hard at her food. The harder she stared, the bigger it seemed to grow. "Gosh," she said, "there must be a whole forest of broccoli here."

As she spoke, Baby Piggy imagined what it would be like to shrink…and shrink…and shrink…until she was a teeny tiny piggy, no longer than a minute, no bigger than a thimble, no louder than a baby's whisper, standing in the middle of a vast green forest of broccoli.

"Oh, dear!" squeaked tiny Baby Piggy.

Suddenly she heard voices. She made her way to a clearing in the

forest, and there she found her nursery pals, Skeeter and Scooter.

"What are you doing here?" Skeeter asked.

"What do you mean, what am I doing here? This is *my* broccoli forest, and as soon as I find my way through it, I'm going to the chocolate pudding pond."

"So are we," said the twins. "We'll help you out of the broccoli forest if you'll help us tame the macaroni monsters. Then we can all go to the pond together."

"It's a deal," said Piggy.

Using their forks, they cleared a path through the thick forest of broccoli. It was hard work, but the delicious thought of the chocolate pudding pond kept them going.

At last the Babies came to the edge of the forest. They were just catching their breath when who should they see but the macaroni monsters! They were tall and wiggly and extremely squiggly, and looked completely impossible to tame.

"They're afraid of spoons," Scooter whispered.

So the intrepid three put away their forks, took up their spoons, and faced the macaroni monsters.

"All right, macaroni monsters," said Baby Piggy. "Prepare to meet your doom—I mean spoon."

The Babies scooped and spooned and ladled and shovelled, and after a very long struggle they managed to make noodle pudding out of those macaronis. Then they sat down to rest.

"Whew!" said Piggy. "I really could eat a spoon of chocolate pudding right now."

"What's that over there?" asked Scooter.

"Maybe chocolate pudding," said Skeeter hopefully.

The three Babies got to their feet and headed toward the shiny something that looked as if it just might be chocolate pudding.

"It's certainly not pudding," Skeeter said when they got there.

"I'd say it's a river," said Scooter.

"If you ask me," said Piggy, looking down into it, "it's a pretty weird colour for a river."

But it *was* a river, a pinkish-reddish river that was very wide and flowing along ever so swiftly.

Just as they were wondering how in the world they would get across it, they heard a familiar voice singing:

"Oh, slurp your soup right through a straw.
Why use a spoon? There is no law.
Soup to slurp. It's so much fun.
Munch that bread when you're done!

"Hi, there!" said Kermit. "Won't you join me?"

Sure enough, there was Baby Kermit floating down the tomato soup river on a barge made from a slice of bread. The three Babies clambered aboard and took turns with the straw. When they had slurped the river dry and munched up the entire barge, Piggy sat on the riverbank and told Kermit all about the chocolate pudding pond that awaited them at the end of their journey.

"Chocolate pudding!" shouted Kermit. "Why didn't you say so? I love ponds and I love pudding. Can I come too?"

"Of course!" the others said. Together, the four set off through the countryside until they came to a lumpy white range of mountains.

"These must be the mashed potato peaks that Fozzie's always talking about," said Kermit.

Then they heard yodelling and saw a skier swoop down the spuddy slopes toward them.

"That must be Fozzie," said Piggy.

"At your service," said Baby Fozzie, schussing to a stop before them.

"Gosh, Fozzie," said Kermit. "Those mountains look awfully high to me."

"And lumpy," said the twins, shaking their heads.

"And bumpy," said Piggy.

"I'll be happy to guide you across," said the cheerful mountaineer. "Just strap on your skis and follow me."

Before they knew it, the Babies were standing at the summit of the highest mashed potato peak. Fozzie pointed out the chocolate pudding glistening in the not-too-far distance. All they had to do now, he explained to them, was get through the asparagus fields, and they would be knee-deep in chocolate.

"Follow me," said Fozzie.

Then down the mountain, *whoooooooosh!* They all skied.

But when they got to the bottom, they saw that the asparagus fields were far thicker than they had appeared to be from the top of the mountain. Even cheery Fozzie looked disappointed. Then they heard a strange squawking noise coming from deep in the fields.

"Hi-ho, Ketchup, away!"

Through the fields of asparagus Baby Gonzo came galloping, mounted on a most peculiar-looking steed.

"Whoa, Ketchup. Whoa, boy!" The horse slid to a halt and immediately began to graze on the asparagus growing all around.

"Something tells me you friends are down on your luck," Baby Gonzo said.

"How can you tell?" Baby Piggy asked.

"The asparagus have ears," Gonzo replied.

"Hey," said Fozzie, "corn has ears, and I'm the one who makes the jokes around here."

"Sorry," said Gonzo. "I'm the Lone Gonzo, and I'll be pleased and proud to take you good folks through the asparagus fields. Climb onto my trusty steed, Ketchup."

Bravely, the five Babies climbed onto the strange beast's back.

"Giddy-up, Ketchup!" said the Lone Gonzo. Then off they went, galloping right through the thick fields of asparagus.

"I can smell the pudding now!" sighed Baby Piggy.

"Me too," said Skeeter and Scooter.

"There it is!" said Kermit.

"My mouth is watering," said Piggy.

Just as they got to the edge of the pond, trusty Ketchup spied a last tasty patch of asparagus. He pulled up short and sent all six Babies flying smack into the middle of the chocolate pudding pond. *Splat!*

"Whoopee!" they yelled. "Thank you, Nanny!"

"You're welcome, children."

Nanny's voice brought Piggy back to normal size again. There she stood by the nursery table. Outside the window the sky was blue, the birds were chirping, and the squirrels were scampering to and fro. On the plate before Piggy was a big bowl of yummy, delicious chocolate pudding.

"You were all so good," Nanny went on. "You ate every single thing on your plates."

"That's because we shared," explained Piggy.

"We each had a little of everything," said Kermit.

"And we made a game out of it," said Gonzo.

"Enjoy your pudding," said Nanny, turning to leave. "You deserve every mouthful."

"Yes, we really do," said Piggy.

So, spoons in hand, the Muppet Babies dived into their dessert and ate every last drop of that chocolate pudding—without any trouble whatsoever!

SPOT THE DIFFERENCE

Colour these drawings and see if you can find 5 differences in them.

FANCY DRESS

For a party, Baby Kermit is dressed up as a king. Scooter isn't ready yet, but he does know what he is going dressed as. See if you can guess what he is going as.

a coweboy

60

THE MATCH GAME

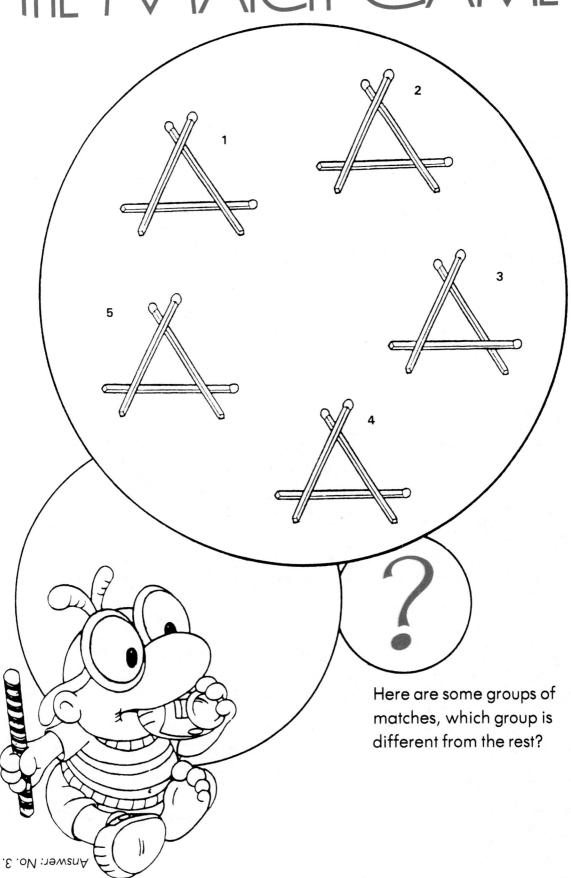

Here are some groups of matches, which group is different from the rest?

Answer: No. 3.